KIDS CAN'T STOP READING
THE CHOOSE YOUR
OWN ADVENTURE® STORIES!

"Choose Your Own Adventure is the best thing that has come along since books themselves."

—Alysha Beyer, age 11

"I didn't read much before, but now I read my Choose Your Own Adventure books almost every night."

—Chris Brogan, age 13

"I love the control I have over what happens next."

—Kosta Efstathiou, age 17

"Choose Your Own Adventure books are so much fun to read and collect—I want them all!"

—Brendan Davin, age 11

And teachers like this series, too:

"We have read and reread, worn thin, loved, loaned, bought for others, and donated to school libraries our Choose Your Own Adventure books."

CHOOSE YOUR OWN ADVENTURE®—
AND MAKE READING MORE FUN!

Bantam Books in the Choose Your Own Adventure® series
Ask your bookseller for the books you have missed

PLAYOFF CHAMPION

BY FELIX VON MOSCHZISKER

ILLUSTRATED BY HAL FRENCK

An R. A. Montgomery Book

BANTAM BOOKS
NEW YORK · TORONTO · LONDON · SYDNEY · AUCKLAND

RL4, age 10 and up

PLAYOFF CHAMPION

A Bantam Book/May 1993

*CHOOSE YOUR OWN ADVENTURE® is a registered
trademark of Bantam Books,
a division of Bantam Doubleday Dell Publishing Group, Inc.
Registered in U.S. Patent and Trademark Office and elsewhere.*

*Original conception of Edward Packard
Cover art by Bill Dodge
Interior illustrations by Hal Frenck*

ISBN 0-553-56000-X

Published simultaneously in the United States and Canada

*Bantam Books are published by Bantam Books, a division of
Bantam Doubleday Dell Publishing Group, Inc. Its trademark,
consisting of the words "Bantam Books" and the portrayal of a
rooster, is Registered in U.S. Patent and Trademark Office and
in other countries. Marca Registrada. Bantam Books, 1540
Broadway, New York, New York 10036.*

PRINTED IN THE UNITED STATES OF AMERICA

OPM   0 9 8 7 6 5 4 3 2 1

Dedicated to
my beloved Sharon

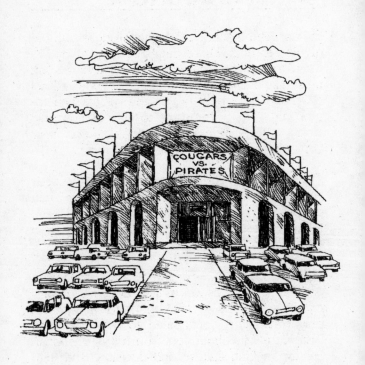

WARNING!!!

Do not read this book straight through from beginning to end. These pages contain many different adventures that you may have when you must take over as player-manager of your school baseball team—right before the national championship game. From time to time as you read along, you will be asked to make a choice. Your choice may lead to success or disaster!

The adventures you have are the results of your choices. You are responsible because you choose. After you make a decision, follow the instructions to find out what happens to you next.

Think carefully before you act. Baseball is a game of strategy as well as skill, and your team is counting on you to lead them to victory. As player-manager, you'll need to think fast and keep your wits about you. You will be responsible for making split-second decisions that ultimately may mean the difference between triumph and defeat.

Good luck!

You are the best catcher your school's baseball team, the Wynona Cougars, has had in a long time. You are also one of the best hitters on the team. Your skills are about to be put to the ultimate test, because the Cougars are set to play in the biggest game of their lives, the semifinal game of the National Invitational Tournament. If you win, the team will go on to the finals and a shot at the national championship. Making it this far has taken plenty of excellent playing and teamwork, and you and the rest of the Cougars have met every new challenge under the guidance of your beloved coach, Skipper Farrow. Coach Farrow has taught you everything he's learned in a lifetime dedicated to baseball. His leadership has had as much to do with the team's reaching the semifinals as has the considerable talent of the team.

Still, in this game your team is the underdog. The opposition, the powerful Passyunk Timber Wolves, pulverized their opponents in the elimination rounds, scoring forty-six runs in six games and giving up only three.

It's less than an hour to game time. You are standing near the dugout chatting with your center fielder Brenda Gorczyk. Suddenly you hear harsh coughing behind you. You and Brenda whirl around and see that Coach Farrow has fallen to the grass and is clutching his chest, his face an ugly grayish color.

"Oh, no," you exclaim. "Get a doctor!"

"Quick!" Brenda cries. "It must be his heart!"

Turn to page 2.

2

The next thirty minutes pass in a blur. An ambulance arrives and medics gently lift Coach Farrow onto a stretcher and load it into the back of the ambulance. You and your teammates can't believe what has happened. You are even more stunned when a tournament official comes over to tell you that the game must continue as scheduled.

"What?" exclaims your pitcher, Tully Burke, in disbelief. "You've got to be kidding. You can't really expect us to play under these circumstances."

"I'm very sorry," replies the official, a gray-haired man in a business suit. "I know you're all very concerned about Mr. Farrow. But this game is being nationally televised. If you can't play today, you'll forfeit and lose your chance to go on to the finals."

"But how can we play without a coach?" Brenda asks.

"One of you will have to act as player-manager," the official says. He glances at his watch. "The game will begin in about twenty minutes. Good luck to you all. May the best team win." With that, he strides away toward one of the TV cameras near the opposing team's dugout.

You turn to your teammates. "Well, what should we do?"

Go on to the next page.

"Let's go back to the locker room and choose a player-manager," suggests Wendy Ruhk, another of the team's star hitters, who plays first base like a pro. "That's the only thing to do."

"Wendy's right," says shortstop Brian Chavez. "The game must go on. We owe it to the Skipper."

In the locker room, there is a quick vote. You are unanimously elected to be emergency player-manager. It is a great responsibility, but the choice is really no surprise. As the catcher, you handle the ball frequently, and you decide on each pitch with the pitcher. What's more, because you are the only player positioned to face the whole field all at once, you direct and lead the defense. For a catcher, leadership is a job requirement.

Your new job begins within moments of the election. Another official comes up to you in the clubhouse and says, "We can't find the lineup card for your team. It must have been in Mr. Farrow's pocket when they took him to the hospital."

"I'll take care of it," you say.

Turn to page 17.

When it's your turn at bat in the bottom of the fourth inning, you finally manage to make solid contact with one of Clinton's sinkers. The ball feels as though it's made of lead, and it goes straight to the shortstop for an easy out. As you walk back to the dugout, your hands are stinging from the impact of the pitch.

The game is still scoreless. Then Scarboro starts a rally during their next turn at bat. Bye Bye Biner leads off with a single to center field. Next, Joe Scover smacks the ball right past Rhubarb on second. Your center fielder, Byron Bucklew, scoops it up on the second bounce. Meanwhile, Biner takes second.

Two on and no outs. The Scarboro manager is standing in front of the dugout with one foot on the top step. He wipes his shin, claps his hands twice, and tugs the bill of his cap.

Out on second base, Biner kicks the dirt and dusts off his hands. It looks as though they're making signs. Good Dog McGee is at bat now. He is looking back at his dugout. This might be a bunt.

It is. McGee hits a beautiful drag bunt that stops dead four feet out from the plate near the third base line. You grab it and throw him out at first, but the runners advance to second and third. One away.

Turn to page 51.

You hand the umpire the card with the left-handed batters in the lineup. Then you head back to your dugout along the first base line. Passyunk is up first, so you won't know whether you made the best decision until you have retired the side.

As you're strapping on your chest protector and shin guards, you glance across at Passyunk's on-deck circle. The leadoff hitter for the Timber Wolves is there, swinging a black bat with a big weight ring on the end. It's Gar Deetstrom. You've heard he's a notorious first-ball hitter.

You take your place behind the plate. Tully throws a couple of last-minute warm-up pitches, and Deetstrom puts down the black bat and heads toward the batter's box.

"Play ball!" shouts the ump. You signal for a curve ball. Deetstrom swings on the first pitch and connects, sending the ball rocketing into deep center field, about twenty feet behind the regulation eight-foot padded fence they put up for the tournament. Byron Bucklew, one of the lefties you decided to play, goes back against the fence and jumps. But it's a waste of time—the hit is a home run. Passyunk takes the lead, 1–0.

The next batter for the Timber Wolves is Augie Colt, a little guy with broad shoulders. Tully is so shaken up from the leadoff home run that he hits Colt in the rib cage with a slider. There are catcalls from the Passyunk dugout as Augie takes his base.

Turn to page 54.

After that, everything seems to go your way. In the second half of the first inning, the Cougars get four runs, thanks in part to big hits by left-handed batters Byron Bucklew and Charlene Schillhammer. In the second inning you add six more runs. By the eighth inning the score is 18–1 in your favor.

During the top of the ninth inning, Coach Farrow is wheeled into the dugout in a wheelchair. A cheer goes up from the entire team. The coach gives a thumbs-up sign and a weak grin.

A few minutes later Tully strikes out the third Passyunk batter in a row, ending the game. You and the other Cougars are jubilant as you rush over to greet Coach Farrow. However, the good news that he is going to be okay is tempered by bad news: the doctors are insisting that he stay in bed and rest for at least a month. He won't be able to lead the team through the championship game. In fact, he'll be lucky if the doctors even let him come and watch.

Your teammate T. T. Chalmers slaps you on the back. "Looks like you'd better not hang up your manager's hat yet, my friend," he says.

Coach Farrow nods and looks you straight in the eye. "You did a fine job out there today, kid," he says in a shaky voice. "If you keep up the good work, there's no reason why the Cougars can't be national champs."

You swallow hard. You hope you're up to the challenge. The whole team is counting on you.

Turn to page 84.

8

Cecil is up next. If anyone can do it, he can. He smacks a line drive to shallow right. Turner races in and grabs it on one hop. It's a single—and Muskrat scores! Everyone leaps up and piles out of the dugout to celebrate. Out on the base path, Fargo begins doing an exuberant victory dance.

Everyone thinks you have won the game. But something is wrong in your mind. You're not sure what it is until you see Turner sneaking toward Fargo, who didn't bother to touch second when he saw the winning run come in. Suddenly you realize that the run doesn't count if the third out in the inning is a force-out. And since Fargo never bothered to touch second, he still can be forced!

Turn to page 27.

10

This is the moment of truth for a catcher. As the throw comes in, you can see out of the corner of your eye that Turner is closing in fast. It's going to be close. A collision is unavoidable—Turner is small, but she's a tough and fearless ballplayer.

You block the plate, crouching low, and concentrating on catching the ball and then squeezing it just as Coach Farrow taught you. The ball smacks into your mitt. You have just a fraction of a second to squeeze it when Turner blasts into you like a runaway truck. The impact flips you over backward, your legs in the air and your face in the dirt. There's dust in your eyes. Your ears are ringing. You feel sand in your mouth and come up spitting.

The umpire is signaling safe. You look in your mitt. The ball is gone! But where? Murtha, who is rounding third, sees your confusion and charges down the line, trying for another score.

Frantically, you look this way and that. You see Wendy pointing a few feet to your left. She's screaming at you. You look over and spot the ball. As you jump on it, Murtha starts his slide. You dive toward him, but you're too late. It's 5–5 with no outs. And Biner, the lead run, is on second base.

Turn to page 55.

Bad Dog flies out to second on the third pitch. Tully walks Darryl Vooch, but Clinton strikes out to end the inning.

Clinton's sinker ball continues to frustrate your batters in the next two innings. Muskrat Henderson grounds out. Then Tully hits an easy fly ball to Scover. Cecil strikes out. T.T. strikes out. You ground out. Brian strikes out. At the end of the seventh inning, Clinton has retired eleven of your batters in a row. But Tully has been holding his own, and Scarboro hasn't been able to score either.

As you're heading out of the dugout to start the eighth inning, Cecil turns to you. "There has to be a way to win this game."

Wendy nods. "We can't give up yet. This Clinton guy isn't a machine. He's got to mess up eventually." She pretends to swing. "And when he does, we'll be ready."

"Definitely," T.T. puts in. "But the key word now is defense."

"That's right," you say. "We've got to keep them from scoring. If they can't get a run, Clinton's pitching won't help them a bit."

"All right," Cecil says with a grin. "Let's go do it, Cougars!"

Turn to page 61.

Wendy catches the ball and fires to second well ahead of Bad Dog. Bad Dog throws on the brakes and heads back to first. He's caught in a rundown. He wheels and dodges and cuts, but gradually the infielders close in. When Wendy finally applies the tag, she knocks Bad Dog flat on his rear end.

When it's all over and Bad Dog is walking back to the dugout, you suddenly realize that his brother, Good Dog, is just a couple of feet away from you, standing on home plate! He must have snuck home during the rundown when everyone else in the park was watching Bad Dog. Even the umpire is surprised. But the run counts, and the score is 4–0.

Turn to page 95.

You know just the player you want to replace Brenda with—the backup catcher, Mitchell Pond. Mitch is a superfast runner, and he's got the best arm on the team. The only trouble is, he can't hit. The thought of putting him in for Brenda when she's on a roll is a little frightening. Brenda is due up in the bottom of the inning, and you may need her bat.

There's one other solution. You could put Mitch in for T.T. in right field. With his extra foot speed, Mitch might be able to make some plays in the fringes of Brenda's territory in center field. That way you'd still be able to take advantage of Brenda's batting skill.

If you send Mitch in for T.T.,
turn to page 111.

If you decide to substitute Mitch for Brenda,
turn to page 70.

T.T.'s run puts the score at 3–1 with the bases loaded and one out. Cecil comes up and hits one right to Scover at short. The runners don't move. Two away.

Brenda is up next. She takes two strikes and then hits the ball way out into the gap in right center. Turner and Biner converge as they go after the ball. Turner just manages to touch the ball with her glove, deflecting it up and over Biner's head. The ball bounces onto the warning track and back, finally coming to rest against the fence.

The crowd is screaming. Muskrat and Brian are crossing the plate. Tully is not far behind. Biner races back to get the ball. He reaches it just as Brenda rounds third. He whirls and fires.

It's a strong throw, but not strong enough. The ball bounces once by the mound. Pirates catcher Darryl Vooch runs out to meet it just as Brenda crosses the plate. It's an inside-the-park grand-slam home run! The Cougars lead 5–3.

As the pandemonium dies down, the Scarboro manager replaces Clinton with a new pitcher named Lionel Bax. You're the next batter, and you soon find out that Bax throws an incredible looping curve. He strikes you out in three pitches.

Turn to page 110.

16

Both Santucci at second and Scover at short-stop are frozen in position as the ball whistles directly over the bag at second hardly eight feet off the ground. But not Biner. He just snatches it out of the air about forty feet behind the bag, barely breaking stride. Brenda is out instantly. Biner's momentum carries him directly to second base just steps away.

Brian, who was on second, is almost to third by now. With his back to center field he is unaware that Biner has unexpectedly charged and caught the ball. He is doubled out the moment Biner's foot touches the bag.

Wendy is halfway to second when Biner catches the ball. She alone of the base runners can see what's happening. She skids to a stop and turns around.

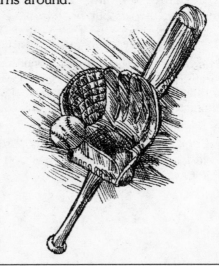

Turn to page 25.

But you know that coming up with a starting lineup won't be that easy. The pitcher for the Timber Wolves is the dangerous Claude Hackmore. You've heard that he has an overwhelming slider and a split-fingered fastball that drops like an anvil the instant it crosses the plate. When he has to, which isn't often, he also throws a wicked soft curve.

But the worst part is that Hackmore is right-handed, just like all your best hitters. Your right-handed hitters are powerful, but they've had trouble in the past with guys like Hackmore. Your lefties aren't quite as good, but they might make out better just because they're left-handed. Hackmore's right-handed pitches would break right toward them, giving them a definite advantage. Just two more lefties in the lineup might make all the difference—assuming any of your batters can make contact with Hackmore's pitches.

You need some time to turn the question over in your mind. Meanwhile, you make out two different lineup cards and stuff them into your hip pocket. It's almost game time.

Turn to page 108.

Most pitchers know not to throw to an empty base, but Clinton's body is working faster than his mind. So he spins and fires over the head of shortstop Scover, who is also screaming by now. The ball sails into center field. By this time Percy is rounding third base. Even as he slows to a walk, panting and red-faced, you know he's going to score the winning run. You and your teammates pile out of the dugout to meet him at the plate and carry him around the field in triumph. Thanks to Percy, the Cougars are the national champions!

The End

You decide to stick with your right-handed power lineup. After you give the card to the umpire, you head back down to the dugout to strap on your catcher's gear. Passyunk bats first.

"Ready to go?" you ask Tully as the two of you head out of the dugout together.

"Ready as I'll ever be," he replies confidently.

You're glad to see that Tully is in good spirits. Batters have a hard time getting a hit when Tully's on his game. He doesn't have an overpowering fastball, but he does have a curve and a decent slider, and he has three or four different speeds for everything he throws. He beats batters by keeping them off balance and messing up their timing.

In the first inning, the Timber Wolves go down 1–2–3 on two pop flies and a short foul ball over by the dugout that Wendy Ruhk picks up without any trouble. Tully's looking good!

Unfortunately, when the Cougars come up to bat, Claude Hackmore looks pretty good, too. Cecil Denby gets on base with a skimpy little infield single that no one but he could have been fast enough to beat out. But then T. T. Chalmers hits into a double play and Rhubarb Channing flies out to left.

After that, the score stays 0–0 for inning after inning. Hackmore strikes out sixteen of your batters, nine in a row at one point.

Turn to page 91.

Fargo's face lights up. "Cool! I'm plenty ready to win this baby and go down in pinch-hitting history." He jumps to his feet, almost tripping over reserve infielder Dabney Chu's feet. "Hey, Dabney, *amigo,* where's my lucky bat?" He digs through the pile of extra bats until he finds a bright blue aluminum one with a wildly patterned purple and green grip. "Aha, here it is." He grabs the bat in both hands and rushes out of the dugout.

You glance at Dabney and laugh, shaking your head. Fargo is a real character. He's also an instinctive hitter, but he doesn't have much baseball sense. If the game goes to extra innings, you'll have to send in your reserve pitcher, Wishbone Walker. Still, all you need to win is one run. You hope Fargo can deliver.

On Bax's second pitch, Fargo smacks a beautiful single to right. Brenda sees her chance and dashes home from second as if her life depended on it. Muskrat makes it to third. The crowd goes wild. The score is tied!

Turn to page 8.

The championship game takes place two days later. Tully is pitching better than ever. He strikes out the first Scarboro batter and walks the next. The two batters up after him hit harmless groundouts to end the first half of the inning.

As soon as Clinton starts pitching, you can see that he's just as good as you've heard he is. He strikes out T.T. and Rhubarb on three pitches each.

You're up next. As you take your place in the batter's box, you wonder what it is he's throwing. It must be pretty tough—T.T. and Rhubarb are two of your best hitters.

Clinton throws two fast strikes before you even get a chance to swing. He's throwing his famous sinker ball—the pitches are down low on the outside of the plate, and they're incredibly fast.

You crowd in for the third pitch. It's low again and misses the outside corner, a ball. You wonder whether he'll dare try you low and away again. You think you just might get a piece of the ball if you concentrate completely on that part of the strike zone.

Go on to the next page.

Of course, he could be setting you up. He has to figure that you're getting the range by now. He's already thrown three sinkers. He must know that a fourth would be suicidal. On the other hand, it might be the very last thing anyone would expect. One more strike and you're out. You step out of the batter's box to think it over.

If you decide to look for the low sinker, turn to page 92.

If you try to be ready for anything, turn to page 50.

Biner's momentum carries him across second toward home. Attempting to achieve a triple play, he leaps into the air and throws across his body toward first. Wendy is running hard, her head down. When she's within range, she hurls herself forward, diving headlong at the base. But she's a split second too late—Murtha has leaned forward and caught the ball, and Wendy is out. The game is over. As it turns out, Wendy breaks her wrist and a couple of ribs in the slide. Even though you lose the game, the dramatic ending is something that will be talked about for years to come.

The End

"Leave it alone, Mitch!" you scream at the top of your lungs. "It's going foul!"

Mitch half turns toward you, looking confused. You realize that he probably couldn't hear what you said. He may even have thought you were yelling for him to catch the ball! You have a feeling you may just have made a big mistake. Your heart is in your throat. If Mitch catches this foul, Santucci will be able to tag up and score easily.

You almost can't bear to watch as Mitch goes up against the railing and reaches over the crowd for the ball. Several spectators are straining for it along with him. Mitch falls over the railing and into the crowd with his glove outstretched. Oh, no, it looks as if he caught the ball!

All of a sudden, a huge figure from a couple of rows back plunges into the small cluster of fans around Mitch. It's a fat spectator with muttonchop whiskers, wearing a Yankees cap. He dives in Mitch's direction and comes up holding the ball. Then he leaps awkwardly down onto the playing surface and lumbers onto the grass of the outfield with a bellow, holding the ball aloft triumphantly.

The stands are in chaos. Out on third base, Santucci tags up and comes running in to score. The umpire signals safe with hands outstretched. But you hardly notice.

Turn to page 80.

You scream at him, but the noise is too great and he doesn't hear you. When Turner finally tags him, Fargo just keeps dancing. He doesn't even realize he is out! The second-base umpire, who has been following everything in spite of the wild celebration, has to tap the dancing Fargo on the shoulder and tell him that he's out and the run doesn't count.

When Fargo realizes what has happened, he collapses onto the ground, looking as if he's going to cry. The rest of you feel the same way. The anticlimax was just too much of a blow.

As if sensing your demoralization, Scarboro strikes in the top of the tenth for two quick runs. Before your team can get it together, you're down 3–1. You recover enough to score a run in the bottom of the inning, but the deficit is just too much to overcome. You lose 3–2.

The End

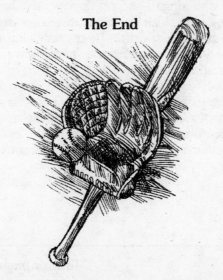

You can't pass up this chance to try the blind pickoff. Taking off your mask, you pretend to wipe some sweat from your forehead. Then you put the mask back on and tap it twice with the palm of your hand. Out at shortstop, Brian pulls on the bill of his cap. So does Tully. The play is on!

Of course, out at second base, Biner has noticed none of this. He's probably still thinking about the inside-the-park home run he almost had.

You go into your crouch, pretend to give a signal, and then thump your mitt three times. On the third thump, Brian and Tully will both be counting. At exactly the same time, you make a target and start to count yourself.

What happens next depends on lots of practice as well as split-second timing. Just as Tully goes into his stretch, Brian breaks for second behind the unsuspecting Biner, who is a good twelve feet off the bag. In the same instant, Tully whirls and throws.

Too late, Biner realizes what is happening. He dives frantically for second, but Brian is there first with the ball. It's a perfect blind pickoff! You and your teammates wave bye-bye to Bye Bye Biner as he heads back to the dugout, scowling.

Turn to page 77.

The next batter for Scarboro is Santucci, but all he can manage this time is a long fly to Cecil in left field. The side is over.

The new pitcher for Scarboro is named Lionel Bax. He's got a good curve, but he's no Clinton. As if to prove that point, Brian takes the first pitch and smashes a hard liner right over Santucci's head. Out in right field, Turner takes two steps and snags the ball easily.

It's an easy out for Scarboro, but it certainly is a relief to see a well-hit ball after eight innings of frustration. The trouble is, the bottom of the order is coming up, with one out. Wendy is up next. She can hit with the best of them on a good day, but it hasn't been a very good day for her so far. Sure enough, she strikes out. But then Brenda surprises everybody by smacking a sizzling single into the gap between first and second, and you have a runner on base with two outs.

Muskrat is up next. Bax walks him, anticipating the bottom of the order. Tully is due up next. You turn to Fargo Yates. "I'm sending you in to bat for Tully. Think you're ready?"

Turn to page 21.

Wildly, you wave Cecil in with both hands. He breaks for home. Clinton is covering home plate for Vooch. Vooch finally gets the ball, and throws to Clinton. Cecil knows just what to do. He drops his shoulder and barrels right into Clinton, knocking him on his rear end before he can even catch the ball. T.T. goes to third on the play. Your split-second thinking paid off!

The score is now 2–1. But even more importantly, you got a chance to break Clinton out of his groove.

There's still a runner on third and only one out as you resume your turn at bat. Clinton is definitely rattled. You bang his next pitch into left field for a single, sending T.T. home. The score is tied, 2–2.

Brian hits a long fly to right for the second out. Then Wendy homers over the right field wall. The ball soars way up and hangs there as it catches the wind, then drops just over the fence as right fielder Toyota Turner watches helplessly.

Turn to page 63.

You can't hold your anger in for one more second. You throw your mask all the way out to the pitcher's mound, and you're just about to give the ump a big piece of your mind when the first-base umpire comes running up.

"The kid's right," the first-base ump says breathlessly. "That fielder never had possession of the ball. The moment the guy in the Yankees cap touched it, the ball was dead. The runner can't advance. He has to return to third base."

You turn to the home plate ump and say, "See? I'm glad *someone* knows the rules of this game."

"That's enough of your attitude!" roars the ump. "Yer outta here!" He points to your dugout.

Turn to page 44.

T.T. gives chase, but the ball is in foul territory now, skipping along the low railing in front of the box seats. Meanwhile Murtha is crossing the plate. Biner has just rounded second base when a fan, a big fat guy wearing a Yankees hat, leaps over the railing and pounces on the ball.

He jumps up, waving his prize. The stands erupt in laughter and applause just as Biner comes pounding across the plate with a big grin on his face, clearly thinking he has hit an inside-the-park home run.

However, when the applause dies down, the ump declares a ground rule double. Murtha's run counts, but Biner is returned to second base.

Biner shrugs and grins. He jogs back out to second and immediately takes a big lead. Suddenly, you remember something that Coach Farrow always told you—the opposition is most vulnerable at its moments of greatest success.

This might be just the right time for a blind pickoff, you think. If it's successful, you'll get rid of a dangerous runner in scoring position and kill the Scarboro rally. But the blind pickoff is risky. If Tully throws the ball away, Biner could score, and you'd be down 2–0.

If you want to try the blind pickoff,
turn to page 28.

If you decide to play it safe,
turn to page 86.

Tully's face has convinced you that he can still do the job, and you leave him in the game. But he has some trouble with Good Dog McGee. The count runs up to 3–2. You signal for the knuckleball and hold your breath.

The pitch comes in inside. Good Dog McGee connects with a sharp line drive down the third base line. Muskrat lunges and makes a miraculous catch. As he recovers himself, he notices Biner has gone several steps off the bag. Before Biner can return, Muskrat steps on third and fires the ball to Wendy at first base, beating Scover's return by a half step.

It's a triple play, and the inning is over, with the score tied at 5–5.

There is no score in the bottom of the ninth. You finally bring in Wishbone Walker to relieve Tully at the top of the tenth inning. He strikes out the side and gets a big hand from the crowd. Neither team manages to score in the tenth or the eleventh innings, nor the twelfth or the thirteenth.

In the fourteenth inning Muskrat triples off the left field wall, but he stands stranded on the bag for the rest of the inning as Clinton strikes out the next two batters and retires the third on an easy fly to center field. By the bottom of the sixteenth inning it's obvious that everyone on both teams is dog tired. You have used up all of your reserve players by now. All but one, that is. It's the perfect time to send in Percy Manwaring.

Turn to page 48.

You're not sure exactly what happens next. But when you watch the play later on videotape, it looks something like this:

Tully delivers his pitch, and Murtha connects. At exactly the same moment, Cecil takes a step backward and accidentally lands on a pigeon. The bird flies up and spooks all the pigeons on the fence. They take off in the direction of home plate.

Meanwhile, the ball that Murtha hit is coming toward them. Some people think it would have been a double. Personally, you think it had home run written all over it.

Whatever the case, it's a high solid blast that's going to bring in some runs. It flies right into the flock of pigeons. WHOCK! Feathers spray out all over the place, and suddenly the ball is dropping out of the cloud of birds and feathers about fifteen feet from Cecil. He runs over, dives . . . and catches the ball! The game is over, and you're the champions—saved by a bird.

The End

You signal for the change-up. Biner takes a healthy cut but misses—strike one. You signal for the same pitch again. However, this time Biner is ready for it. He smacks it with all his might—right at Tully! Tully doesn't even have time to move out of the way. The ball smashes into his right shin, and he's down, howling in pain. You rush out to the mound with the doctor and several other adults right behind you. Biner stands stock-still at the plate, looking shocked.

You reach Tully's side. He is groaning in pain. "Tully! Can you move it?" you ask anxiously. But you don't even need to hear his answer. It's obvious just from looking at his leg that it's badly broken.

Turn to page 89.

You signal for a slider. Tully winds and throws. It's coming in low and over the middle of the plate. Biner swings hard and misses. You fooled him!

Next you signal for a low fastball and make a target on the outside of the plate. Biner swings and misses again. You've got him off balance.

That's two strikes. You decide that it's time to throw something a bit slower. You ask Tully for a curve. Biner connects but fouls into the third-base stands.

You go back to the slider, but this time Biner is ready for it. He smacks a vicious line drive down the third base line. The ball is never more than two feet off the ground. Your third baseman, Muskrat Henderson, dives for it, but he doesn't stand a chance. Biner winds up at second, and the crowd gives him a big hand.

On the very next pitch Biner tries to steal third. Instantly you are up and ready to throw. Should you try to nail him at third? Muskrat and Rhubarb Channing, who is playing second, are in position and ready. But Biner is fast, and the smallest mistake or fumble could give the Pirates another run. You only have a split second to decide what to do.

If you throw to third, turn to page 106.

If you hold the ball, turn to page 64.

"It's that rotator cuff injury," Byron tells you between innings. "I can probably still hit, but my throwing arm's going to be pretty shaky." This is something to worry about. Byron is your number-two batter. You hate to pull him out early in a championship game, especially when you are in need of runs, but you know that keeping him in could make his injury even worse. You do what you know Coach Farrow would have done and pull Byron from the game, putting Brenda in in his place.

This turns out to be a very good decision. Over the next five innings Brenda gets three hits. But unfortunately none of these translates into runs for the Cougars. Neither do hits by Tully, Wendy, Brian, or Cecil. The Pirates manage to foil the Cougars' attempts to score at every turn. And in the fifth inning the Pirates score themselves on a big hit by their star batter, Murtha. The score goes to 3–0.

Wendy is the first batter up at the bottom of the seventh. She hits a pop fly for the first out. Then T.T. and Muskrat get hits, ending up on first and third. Then the Pirates' pitcher, Doorknob Clinton, walks Brian, loading the bases. You know he wants to pitch to Tully with the force-out at every base.

Go on to the next page.

You prepare yourself for the worst. But Tully takes a big swing and hits a dribbler that bounces once and then stops dead eight feet short of the pitcher's mound, faking everybody out. Tully makes it safely to first, and T.T. scores from third.

Turn to page 15.

The next batter, the Timber Wolves' cleanup hitter, Matt Weisenbach, steps up to the plate. In batting practice you saw Weisenbach blast pitch after pitch into the upper deck in left field. You can't throw fastballs to a bomber like that. They go out faster than they come in.

You signal for an outside curveball. Weisenbach swings and misses. That's interesting, you say to yourself. You decide to try another one.

As the pitch approaches the plate, Weisenbach tenses with anticipation, and you're afraid that he's got it figured out. For a split second you sense disaster. Weisenbach grunts as he takes a ferocious cut and misses again. He can't hit the outside curve!

Now you know exactly what to do—call for the same pitch a third time. No one would be crazy enough to do that, which is exactly why it might work.

And it does. The pitch comes in, and Weisenbach misses it by a mile. He throws down the bat in disgust and walks back to the dugout, muttering to himself.

Turn to page 7.

You have no choice but to obey. You run out and grab your mask, then head down the tunnel behind the dugout. You feel horrible. You just hope you haven't blown the game for the rest of the team.

In the clubhouse, you switch on the TV and watch silently. Bye Bye Biner comes up and hits a grounder to first base. Wendy knocks down the ball, and it twists away from her. But she pounces on it and trots to first three steps ahead of Biner, holding her glove triumphantly aloft.

The Cougars won the game anyway! You see your teammates mobbing Wendy out by first base. Your spirits are lifted, and you decide you might as well head back out and join the fun.

The End

A championship is a championship. A couple of years from now, everyone will have forgotten the birds and no one will know the difference. Besides, someone might trip over a bird and get hurt.

"I'll take the shortened game," you say. "For all I know, Cecil could break a leg trying to run the bases with all those pigeons around him." You look at the Scarboro manager. "I hope you're okay with this. Your players are at risk, too, you know."

"You're absolutely right," he says. "I can't complain. We had a good seven-inning game, and you guys were beating us pretty well. I don't mind going down in history as losing to a bunch of pigeons. That's all anyone's going to remember about this game, anyway."

The End

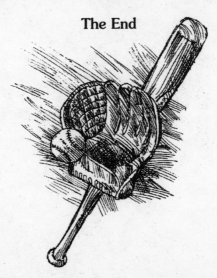

You suspect they are going to bunt this time. Frank Murtha is stepping up to the plate for his turn at bat. Just then Rhubarb catches your eye. You call for a time-out and motion to the infield. Everyone jogs over to the pitcher's mound for a conference.

Rhubarb can hardly wait to speak. "They're going to bunt this time. I know it. Remember when Good Dog McGee did that drag bunt in the fifth inning? Well, I was watching their signs then. It's a bunt this time for sure."

You remember it, too. But you're afraid it might be a trap. What if there was a signal you missed, telling Murtha to disregard the previous signals?

If you tell the team to prepare for a bunt, turn to page 65.

If you tell them you think it's a trap, turn to page 68.

48

Percy is barely four and a half feet tall and weighs 164 pounds, which is a lot for a kid who can barely see over the dashboard of a car. Coach Farrow calls Percy his secret weapon, but he doesn't like to use him except in real emergencies. He says he doesn't want to make a mockery of the game.

In nearly all respects, Percy is a terrible baseball player. He can't throw farther than ten feet or so, and he couldn't get a hit if the ball were the size of a pumpkin. But one day in practice Farrow discovered that Percy was an amazingly talented, though limited, runner. He can run from first to third a full second faster than anyone on the team. After that, he has to sit down and catch his breath.

With all his natural padding, Percy doesn't mind being hit by a pitch if that's what it takes to get on base. But that doesn't happen very much. Because of his ridiculous appearance and tiny strike zone, Percy usually draws a walk. Then he's all set to steal.

Turn to page 98.

Over the next couple of innings, you chip away at the Pirates' lead. In the bottom of the eighth the score is 8–6. You lead off with an infield single. Brian singles you to third, and Wendy walks. The bases are loaded.

You wonder if Wendy's walk means that Clinton is tiring and losing his touch. Brenda comes up and hits a long foul on the first pitch. Then Clinton throws three straight balls. The count is 3–1, with no outs and the bases loaded. This is a big opportunity, maybe the last one you'll get.

Out on third base, you ponder the situation. Should Brenda be swinging at the next pitch or taking it? Clinton has to put it in the strike zone, or he'll walk in a run. You're sure he'll go with his sinker. If Brenda knows it's coming, she can probably put the ball in play, which might score a run—maybe even two. If you signal for her to swing at the next halfway decent pitch, you're pretty sure she'll know to be on the lookout for that sinker.

On the other hand, Clinton also has to get the pitch after *that* over the plate. Maybe it would be better to signal Brenda to wait him out.

*If you signal for her not to swing,
turn to page 82.*

*If you signal for Brenda to swing,
turn to page 103.*

Certain that there's no way Clinton would dare throw the same pitch four times in a row, you step back into the batter's box. Clinton takes a big windup. Your whole body tenses up.

Then he throws. Too late, you realize that it's yet another low sinker. Caught off guard, you swing wildly and miss. Strike three.

That's all for this side. There's no score after one full inning. The second inning is also scoreless, as are the third and fourth. Tully gives up a walk, a double, and two singles, all scattered.

The real story is Clinton, who turns out to be an overpowering sinker-ball pitcher. He gets stronger and stronger the more he throws. A sinker is not hard to hit, but it's very hard to hit well. None of your batters is having much luck with it.

Turn to page 5.

The next batter up is Bad Dog McGee, seventh in the Pirates' batting order and a decent hitter. This gives you a choice. You can have Tully walk him intentionally and load the bases. With the two weakest hitters coming up, you'll have a pretty good chance of getting out of the inning.

Or you can have Tully throw him a bunch of borderline pitches and see if he swings. If he strikes out, so much the better. If he walks, it's not the end of the world. Of course if he hits, you give up one or maybe even two runs.

*If you have Tully pitch to him,
turn to page 11.*

If you signal for a walk, turn to page 58.

52

Rhubarb is up next. Clinton walks him, and you take your place at bat. You decide that desperate times call for desperate measures. On the third pitch, with the count even at 1–1, you see an inside pitch coming. You step into the ball and catch it on your shoulder.

THWUNK! It feels as though you have been kicked by a mule. You clutch your shoulder, breathless with the pain. A doctor runs out onto the field to check you out. Luckily, it's only going to be a bruise. And the important thing is, you're finally on base! You walk out to first and take a lead. Rhubarb advances to second.

Turn to page 112.

54

You call a time-out and head out to the mound to make sure that Tully's all right. He assures you that he'll be fine—he's doing his best to focus and forget about Deetstrom's hit. You jog back to the plate, hoping that he can do it.

Tully throws two low curves to the next Passyunk batter, who hits the second one out to your shortstop, Brian Chavez. Brian flips the ball to your second baseman, who steps on second and fires the ball to first baseman Wendy Ruhk: a double play!

Turn to page 42.

Scover is coming up to bat. He waits out the first two pitches and then blasts a single to right. Biner advances to third. As Good Dog McGee comes up to the plate, you spit out some more sand. Your head is finally starting to clear. You realize that the Pirates are really knocking Tully around. He must be losing his edge. After all, it is the ninth inning.

You wonder about your reserve pitcher, Wishbone Walker. He might be warmed up by now—but then again, he might not. A brand-new fastball pitcher might stop the Pirates in their tracks, but only if he's in top form. Putting Wishbone in right now would be risky, to say the least. With no outs and the Pirates' lead run on third base, you're not sure Tully can get out of this inning without giving up that go-ahead run. Still, the bottom of the Scarboro order is coming up. You can see that familiar look of determination on Tully's face that tells you he's ready to dig in and give it all. Maybe you'd better keep him in the game. You glance from Tully back over to Wishbone in the dugout, weighing the options carefully. The outcome of the game could depend on your decision.

*If you choose to pull Tully,
turn to page 105.*

*If you keep him in the game,
turn to page 35.*

In the fifth inning Rhubarb scores to make it 5–1. The sun is shining, and you're having a good time. It's around this time that you begin to notice the pigeons. Whenever Cecil takes up his position in left field, a whole bunch of pigeons fly down from the crest of the roof of the left field stands and perch on the top of the eight-foot padded fence of the left field wall behind him. Each inning when he takes his position, there seem to be another eight or ten birds out there.

Turn to page 72.

58

You signal for Tully to walk Bad Dog. He does, and the bases are loaded. Darryl Vooch is up next. He hits into a double play to end the inning.

The next couple of innings are a story of frustration. You watch helplessly as Clinton strikes out Brian, Wendy, and Brenda. The side after this goes down in order also. Clinton has now retired twelve batters in a row, and not a ball has been hit out of the infield.

As you walk out to the field to begin the eighth inning, Brian falls into step beside you. "That Clinton guy is a machine," he says. "I've never seen anything like him outside of the majors."

"You're telling me," you say, thinking of that leaden sinker you hit in the fourth inning. "We've really got to keep our defense tight. Sooner or later one of us will figure out how to hit his pitches."

Brian nods. "Then we'll show those Pirates who's boss around here!" He claps you on the shoulder and jogs out to his position at shortstop. You adjust your mask and take your position behind home plate, glancing out to see how Tully is doing. He looks more determined than you've ever seen him.

Go on to the next page.

He gets off to a good start, striking out the first Scarboro batter, Clinton. You grin and give him a thumbs-up. You're glad to see that Clinton isn't as invincible a batter as he is a pitcher. If he were, he'd be downright deadly.

Next at bat is Kayo Santucci. He hits a slow pop fly straight to Brian. Two outs, one to go.

Turn to page 99.

You decide to go for it. You accelerate around second and head for third. The throw must be a trifle wide, because Good Dog is moving up the line a little. Now he's got it and you're sliding. He dives at the bag for the tag—but the umpire signals safe!

Right away, you signal for the suicide squeeze. Brian reaches out half-choked on the first pitch and chops the ball down into the dirt. The ball takes a high, long first bounce as you charge. Kravitz stands around waiting helplessly for it to come down as you cross the plate. You're the champs!

The End

You take your position behind the plate, slightly encouraged by your teammates' optimism. After all, Wendy is right—Clinton is bound to make a mistake sooner or later. Until then, you've just got to continue to keep Scarboro from scoring. "All right, Tully, let's go. You've got an easy out here," you shout as Kayo Santucci steps up to the plate.

Santucci proves you wrong by leading off with a single to left. Toyota Turner is up next, and Tully strikes her out on three pitches. You begin to notice signs being made again in the Scarboro dugout. The manager claps his hands, tugs on his cap, and touches his chin.

Turn to page 47.

Wendy skips and hops for joy as she circles the bases. When she reaches the plate, you're waiting for her, and she slaps your hand for a big high five. You're ahead 4–2.

After that, Clinton settles down and strikes out Brenda to end the side. The game continues with no more scoring until Cecil hits a solo homer in the bottom of the eighth to make it 5–2.

And that's the way it stands going into the top of the ninth. You've got a decent lead. Three more outs and the Cougars will be the national champs!

But first you've got to get by Kayo Santucci, Turner, and Murtha, the top of the Pirates' batting order. It's not going to be easy, you think.

As if to prove you right, Santucci singles and steals second. Tully walks Turner. Then Murtha tops the first pitch, and it takes an erratic, twisting short bounce. Tully manages to knock it down near the mound, but by the time he gets a grip on the ball all three runners are safe. The bases are loaded.

Biner steps to the plate and hits a line drive single to left field. Santucci is over the plate in a flash, and as Cecil charges the ball and makes his throw to the plate, you can see Turner rounding the corner at third and racing down the line toward you.

Turn to page 10.

64

You let Biner steal third base. It's too risky to try to throw him out. Instead, you toss the ball back to Tully, and he pitches to Joe Scover. He bunts, and Biner charges. It's the suicide squeeze! If it's even a halfway decent bunt, he'll score.

It's a lousy bunt. The ball stops about sixteen inches in front of the plate. You just have time to grab it and brace yourself before Biner bowls you over. But you hold on to the ball, and he's out. You jump up and wave the ball triumphantly as Biner slumps back to the dugout and the side is retired. Back in your own dugout, the atmosphere is relaxed and optimistic.

By the third inning, you have tied the score at 1–1. In the fourth inning, you pull ahead 4–1 on a walk, a single by Muskrat, another single by Brian, a successful bunt by Tully, and a double by Cecil Denby.

Turn to page 57.

You tell your teammates to stay at double-play depth but to charge in for the bunt as soon as the pitch is on its way.

As Tully prepares to throw, Murtha is digging in as though he wants to pulverize the ball. It's a pretty good act for someone who's about to bunt, you think.

But it's not an act. Your infielders charge on the first pitch, and Murtha strokes an easy blooper over their heads. He makes it safely to first as Santucci sprints around to third.

Tully is visibly shaken by all this. On the next pitch, Biner hits a double, and both runners come home. The next batter is Scover, who promptly hits a home run.

Now your team has only six outs to score at least three runs against Clinton and his formidable sinker. It turns out to be impossible. Clinton walks Wendy in the eighth inning, but no one else even gets on base. You lose the game 4–0.

The End

You keep silent and you hold your breath as Mitch screeches to a stop five feet inside foul territory and watches as the ball hits the ground, foul by ten feet. You let out your breath in a sigh of relief. You're glad you trusted Mitch to know what he was doing.

On the next pitch, another curveball, Murtha hits a powerful line drive out to right center field. Brenda is lining up to catch it. Oh, no! She'll never make the throw. Suddenly a blur comes in from the right. It's Mitch!

He snatches the ball and fires it off in one stride. It's a 280-foot throw, and the ball never has an arc to it. It comes home to you in a straight line, smacking into your mitt one foot off the ground and just in front of Kayo Santucci's foot as he slides in with what would have been the tying run.

"Yer ou-u-u-t!" cries the umpire. And just like that, the game is over. You leap into the air, waving the ball. The dugout empties. You and your teammates grab Mitch and carry him around the field on your shoulders. The Cougars are the national champions—thanks in large part to your cool head and good decisions!

The End

"Thanks for the info, Rhubarb," you say. "But it just seems too easy to me. I think it's a trap. Let's play at middle depth—make it look like you're ready to charge, but back off quickly as soon as the pitch is on its way."

On the first pitch Murtha pops the ball straight to Wendy, who catches it easily and tags out Santucci as he's returning to base for a double play. You're out of the inning.

Clinton walks Wendy to lead off the bottom of the eighth. She's your first base runner since the fourth inning! Wendy takes a big lead and steals second on the 0–1 count.

On the next pitch, she steals third. You're threatening at last. But one by one Clinton strikes out Brenda, Muskrat, and Tully. The inning ends with the score still 0–0.

"Okay, you can do it, Tully," Cecil says. "You just have to hold them off for one more inning."

"That's right," Wendy says. "Cecil's up first for us in the bottom of the inning. If anyone can beat Clinton's pitching, it's him." She slaps Cecil on the back.

"That's right," Cecil brags. "I'll show those Pirates who's boss."

Go on to the next page.

"I can't wait to see that, Cecil," Tully says with a grin. "I'd better hurry up and retire this side so you can show us."

You're glad to see that your teammates are in such a good mood. You're not feeling much like joking around yourself, though. Even if the Cougars can hold off in the top of the inning, you're not confident that any of you will be able to score against Clinton, even though the top of the order is due up next. Still, you decide to try to remain optimistic. If you pull together as a team, maybe you can still find a way to win. It's not over until it's over.

Turn to page 76.

The only thing that makes you feel safe with this one-run lead is to put Mitch in for Brenda. Mitch is quick and instinctive. He can cover 50 percent more of center field than anyone else on the team. And his arm is a regular cannon. If he could hit, he'd be downright dangerous.

But you don't need to worry about hitting, you think, as you glance at Santucci standing out on second base. Right now, the word is defense.

Toyota Turner tries to bunt. But she hits a little pop-up instead. Tully backpedals off the mound, circles, and grabs it easily. He looks back, but Santucci is holding his base. One out. Tully glances around at his infielders. "That's one, Cougars. Let's get two more!"

Murtha hits a brisk grounder to third. Muskrat looks Santucci back and throws Murtha out at first. That's two outs. Again, Tully turns to face his fielders before pitching. "We only need one more! Let's bear down and finish this thing!"

But bearing down on Biner is not an easy task. He takes a ball and a strike. Then he connects. It's a sharp liner to center—this could be trouble. But Mitch is sprinting in. He dives forward and slides. He's on his belly. The ball is dropping. It's in the webbing of his mitt! He's got it! The game is over! The Cougars are the national champs!

The End

By the seventh inning, there must be almost one hundred pigeons out there, all of them looking at Cecil, flapping their wings, and edging around the way pigeons do. When Cecil goes back to the dugout at the end of each side, they fly back up on the roof.

Then, in the bottom of the seventh, when Cecil goes out to the on-deck circle to get ready to bat, one of the pigeons spots him and flies down from the roof. By the time he's up to bat about thirty of the birds are strutting around the batter's box and walking up the first base line. The umpire calls a time-out and tries to shoo them away, but they keep coming back. A few grounds keepers come out to help him, but they can't get rid of the pigeons either.

Finally Cecil says to the ump, "I don't mind them. They're just my fans. Let 'em be."

The umpire shrugs. "If you say so, Denby. Let's play ball!" Clinton's first pitch is a fastball. Cecil swings and misses, and a couple of pigeons flap into the air, spooked. Then they settle down and go back to milling around. A couple of pitches later, Cecil singles to left, and the pigeons follow him to first base.

The home plate umpire calls you and the Scarboro manager over to discuss the situation. He pulls his rule book out of his hip pocket. "It appears these pigeons are following your left fielder," he says to you. "Has this ever happened before?"

Turn to page 107.

By the end of the eighth inning, Clinton has retired fifteen of your batters in a row. As long as he's on the mound, there doesn't seem to be much hope for your team. Despite your earlier optimism, nobody seems to be figuring out how to hit his vicious pitches.

Vooch hits a long fly out to Brenda in center field to start the top of the ninth. That brings Clinton to the plate. Since he's obviously not much of a hitter, you figure the easiest thing would be to strike him out on three straight fastballs.

But fastballs take a lot of effort, and they've never been Tully's strong point. He's pitched eight long innings, and you're afraid he might be starting to tire. You signal for a fastball anyway. It goes wide—ball one.

Now you're really beginning to worry that a tiring Tully might start missing the plate if you keep asking him for fastballs. You don't want to take the chance of walking Clinton with only one out and the top of the Pirates' order on its way. On the other hand, you also don't want to risk having him get a big hit on an easier pitch. Tully is looking at you expectantly, waiting for your signal.

*If you keep signaling for fastballs,
turn to page 97.*

*If you signal for a knuckleball instead,
turn to page 88.*

"I want to play this one out," you tell the ump.

"So be it," he says. "Let's play ball!"

With the pigeons safely out of the way at first base, Clinton strikes out Byron, and it's your turn to bat.

You step up to the plate determined to do your best to overcome Clinton's pitch, pigeons or no pigeons. You're a little worried about what will happen when Cecil tries to run through all those birds, but you don't have time to think about that now. You just hope he doesn't trip over one of his admirers.

When the pitch comes, it's a perfect curveball. You concentrate, swing—and connect. The ball whizzes out into the first base hole, and Cecil takes off like a shot. Several birds shoot up into the air, flapping their wings. Then, SPLOT! The ball hits a big gray bird. Feathers explode all over the place, and the ball deflects in the direction of the second baseman, Kayo Santucci.

Santucci fields the ball and throws it over to Scover at shortstop. Scover makes the force-out and throws down to Murtha at first. Double play —tough luck! The inning is over.

Nothing gets hit out Cecil's way in the top of the eighth, and he doesn't come up to bat in the bottom of the inning, so the game proceeds without any further trouble from the pigeons.

Turn to page 81.

Tully does his part for the team effort. He works the top of the ninth in six pitches—two groundouts and a long fly ball to center field.

It's the bottom of the ninth with no score. Cecil struts confidently up to the plate, throwing Tully a mock salute. Unfortunately, even Cecil's considerable skills still aren't a match for Clinton's sinker. He's out on a fly to shallow center, which Scover catches easily.

Cecil returns to the dugout shaking his head dejectedly.

"Nice try, Cecil," Brenda says. "That's one of the longest balls anyone's hit off that guy all day."

"Brenda's right, dude. You gave it a shot," Tully says.

Cecil shrugs. "Hey, it's all right. I was just being a nice guy, giving T.T. a chance to be the star," he says good-naturedly.

But apparently it's not T.T.'s turn for stardom either—he strikes out. "Bummer," he says with a deep sigh.

"Nice try," Brenda says again. Nobody else says anything. You can tell that the optimistic mood is wearing off fast.

Turn to page 52.

If you thought the pickoff would slow Scarboro's attack, you were wrong. These guys are winners, or they wouldn't be here. The batter after Biner, Joe Scover, whacks a long fly down the left field line for a home run. You're down 2–0.

In the bottom of the fourth Cecil leads off with a single to center. After a few thwarted attempts, Cecil manages to steal second.

You can tell that Clinton isn't happy about having a runner like Cecil on base. He walks T. T. Chalmers. Then Rhubarb sacrifices to right, moving Cecil to third. You're up next.

Your last time up, Clinton made you ground out on that painful sinker ball. If you hit a grounder now, Cecil will score. Clinton knows this as well as you do, so you figure he'll probably throw you something else. But what?

You're so caught up with thinking about the possibilities that you almost don't notice it when Clinton's first pitch goes into the dirt. It's a wild pitch! It gets by the catcher, Darryl Vooch. He's chasing it. Cecil might be able to score!

Should you wave him in or not? It would be a risky attempt, but you could really use a run right now.

---

*If you decide to wave Cecil home,
turn to page 31.*

*If you decide to wave him back,
turn to page 101.*

This is it. It's now or never if you want to win this game. All you need are two runs, but that seems impossible as long as Clinton is still on the mound.

"What are we going to do? It's not looking good here," T.T. comments as Brian heads out to bat.

You shake your head. "Let's just hope we get a hit."

But you don't. Clinton strikes out Brian in three pitches. Wendy is up next, and the same thing happens to her.

She stomps back into the dugout, looking disgusted. "I can't believe none of us can get a hit," she says. "We're pathetic."

"No, we're not," you say, watching as Clinton strikes out Brenda to end the game. "There's not a kid our age anywhere who could hit against Clinton. He's got an amazing future ahead of him if he stays in this game."

And you're right. The next day, newspapers all over the country are full of accounts of Doorknob Clinton's incredible game. He eventually goes on to the major leagues and has a sensational career, leading the Philadelphia Phillies to three consecutive World Series victories.

The End

The big fan with the Yankees cap is running around in circles out in center field with four blue-shirted security men chasing him. Finally they manage to grab him and drag him off.

It's only then that you notice Santucci's teammates clustered around him, pounding him on the back excitedly. You turn to the umpire. "Wait a minute," you say. "My fielder didn't catch that ball. That run doesn't count!"

"The ball was in the fielder's mitt," says the ump. "That's a catch. The batter is out, and the runner can advance after tagging his base. The score is tied."

All of a sudden you are furious. "But Mitch never had possession of the ball. That big jerk grabbed it. You saw him running around out there!"

Tully is at your elbow. "Take it easy," he says. "He'll throw you out of the game."

It has been a long, hard game. You're not going to give up easily what you and your teammates have struggled so hard to win. You feel an explosion coming on. But a small voice in your head is telling you it might be best to let Tully pull you aside and calm you down.

If you ignore Tully and let off some steam, turn to page 32.

If you decide to back off, turn to page 114.

It's still 5–1 in the top of the ninth when the Scarboro team starts coming to life. First Good Dog McGee walks. Then his brother Bad Dog pops up to first base. After that, Darryl Vooch gets a bloop single, and Clinton whiffs for the second out.

It gets serious a moment later, as Santucci doubles and the score goes to 5–3. Toyota Turner comes to bat, and Tully walks her. Then Murtha steps up to the plate.

You're sure you can make Murtha fly out to left, as he's done several times during the game. You give the signal for an inside change-up, and Tully nods almost imperceptibly.

Out of the corner of your eye, you see Cecil out in left field with all those birds lined up behind him. He knows there's a good chance Murtha's going to hit one out his way, so he's moving back.

The pigeons are shifting around. A couple of them are walking around on the grass behind Cecil. You wonder if he knows they're there. He's got a lot of birds to keep track of.

Turn to page 36.

You signal for Brenda not to swing at the next pitch. She obeys, and it's a ball! Brenda walks, and everyone advances a base. You trot down the line, giving Vooch a cocky grin as you cross home plate. The score is 8–7.

Muskrat comes up to bat next and triples off the fence in right field. There's pandemonium in the dugout as the runners all come home. You're leading by two runs in the bottom of the eighth. You can almost smell the championship.

The Scarboro manager pulls Clinton, replacing him with a huge, dark, scowling guy named Caveman Kravitz. Kravitz strikes out Tully and Cecil on three pitches each. T.T. hits a grounder to the first baseman for the third out.

In the top of the ninth, Biner hits a solo home run to bring the score to 10–9. Scover walks, moves to second on a sacrifice, then steals third. Bad Dog McGee comes up and hits a grounder that takes a weird hop and hits Brian in the forehead. Then it falls in the dirt in front of him. Brian makes the play to first, but Scover scores, tying the game at 10–10.

Turn to page 96.

The final game of the tournament is two days later. You try to ignore the butterflies in your stomach as you size up the opposing team, the Scarboro Pirates. The Pirates are a tough team with no visible weak points—otherwise they wouldn't have made it this far. Still, you're convinced that the Cougars can beat them. Your team is well rested and in good spirits. Coach Farrow is in the stands cheering for you, and your friends and family are all either here or watching on TV. You don't want to let them down.

Tully is even more nervous than you are. He walks the Pirates' first batter, Kayo Santucci.

Next up is Toyota Turner. On Tully's very first pitch to her, Santucci steals second. Turner hits Tully's second pitch for a single, and Santucci coasts home. You're down 1–0. Luckily, the third batter of the inning, Frank Murtha, grounds into a double play. The next batter up is the Pirates' cleanup hitter, Bye Bye Biner, who hit three home runs in their semifinal game of the tournament.

Go on to the next page.

You've heard that Biner is a dangerous pull hitter who likes inside fastballs. This means Tully shouldn't pitch to him on the inside. But your guess is that Biner will lose power if you move the ball farther out over the plate. Since pull hitters are usually fascinated with their own strength and therefore fairly predictable, the most obvious choice would be to give Biner a low outside fastball. But you're not sure Tully can pull that off, especially since he still hasn't quite settled into his rhythm. You decide you'd better try to fool Biner with either a slider or a change-up—two of Tully's specialties. You haven't played against Biner before, so you have no way of knowing which pitch he'll be more likely to fall for. You'll just have to choose one and hope for the best.

If you decide to signal Tully to throw a change-up, turn to page 37.

If you want him to throw a slider, turn to page 39.

You figure the pickoff is too risky. Joe Scover, the next batter, hits a long double to the gap in right center, and Biner scores. It's 2–0.

Tully walks Good Dog McGee, and there are runners on first and second. Then Bad Dog McGee comes up and singles to right. Scover scores, making it 3–0. Good Dog is safe on third.

Bad Dog takes a big lead. Tully throws over to hold him on, and Bad Dog slides back to the bag, spiking Wendy. It looks to you as though he did it on purpose. Wendy limps around in circles for a moment as the doctor comes out to check on her. She has a small gash on her shin, but otherwise she's okay. The game resumes.

Once again, Bad Dog takes a big lead and dances back and forth. Tully throws over to first, and Bad Dog slides back and spikes Wendy again. Now you can see that Wendy is getting angry. Tully looks as though he's getting annoyed, too.

Play resumes once more. Bad Dog takes his lead yet again, so Tully throws over to first one more time. If Bad Dog spikes Wendy again, you know there will be a fight. But Bad Dog doesn't go back. Instead, he breaks for second.

Turn to page 12.

You signal for a knuckleball. Even though he's tired, Tully's breaking stuff apparently is still good. It's so good, in fact, that Clinton misses the knuckler by about a foot.

He looks so ridiculous doing it that you can't resist calling for another one. Clinton swings, and it looks as if he's going to miss it again. But at the last instant the ball takes a dive right into his bat and flies into left for a freak single.

You frown. Things aren't looking good. Santucci is coming to the plate. You call for the knuckler again. Santucci takes a ferocious cut and slams a long high one over Cecil's head in left field. Clinton comes in to score the first run of the game and Santucci holds up with a triple. It's 1–0.

You pull Tully and replace him with your best relief pitcher, Wishbone Walker. Wishbone retires Turner on an infield fly and strikes out Murtha. Then he walks Biner on purpose to pitch to Scover. Scover hits into a force, and you go to the bottom of the ninth.

Turn to page 79.

Minutes later Tully is rushed to the hospital. You and your teammates are standing around on the sidelines talking about Tully when the game official approaches you again. "More tough luck, eh?" he says. However, he doesn't really look very sympathetic. "Listen, kid, like I said before, the game's gotta go on. I know you're all shaken up and everything, but we'd better get moving."

You gather the Cougars around you for a little pep talk, although you're not feeling very optimistic yourself. Play resumes a few minutes later. You send in your reserve pitcher, Wishbone Walker, but it soon becomes apparent that Wishbone is no replacement for Tully. By the fourth inning the Pirates are leading 10–0. And it just keeps getting worse. By the end of the game the score is 19–0. You and your teammates can only watch dejectedly as the Pirates celebrate their new title as national champions.

The End

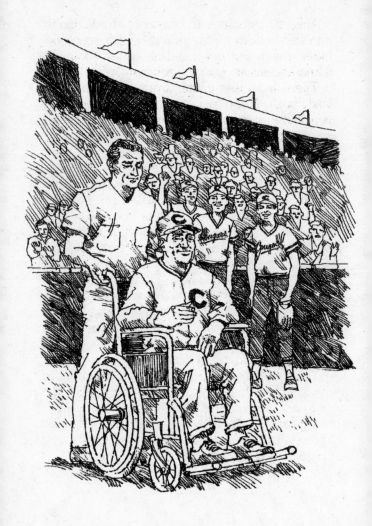

Tully strikes out eight batters himself. Going into the bottom of the ninth, he still has a no-hitter going. But you need to score to win the game and advance in the tournament.

Then there is a clatter from the tunnel that leads back to the locker room. The next thing you know, a green-shirted medic is pushing a wheelchair into the dugout. It's Coach Farrow! He looks exhausted. The medic tells you Coach Farrow can't talk. He can only watch.

But there is a gleam in his eye that inspires the whole team. Rhubarb Channing is the first one up. He hits a triple. You're next. You wait for the ball you want. It comes on the third pitch. You smack a single to right field, and Rhubarb scores. You win the game!

Now there's only one game between you and the national championship. Your opponents are the Scarboro Pirates, and they're going to be a lot tougher than the Timber Wolves. Their pitcher, Doorknob Clinton, is the best pitcher your age anywhere.

You think about trying to find an experienced manager for the championship game, but the rest of the team won't hear of it. After all, you came through in the clutch, and no one else knows the other players like you do. Can you pull off one more miracle?

Turn to page 22.

You decide to look for the sinker. As Clinton takes his windup and delivers, you crowd in, ready to swing right where you hope the pitch is going to be. And sure enough, it's just what you're expecting! You step into the ball and bring your hands around low.

You connect hard, but a shock goes up your arms and into your shoulders. It feels as if you just took a swing at a medicine ball made of iron. The bat splinters and flies out to third with the ball. You manage to make the play close at first, but the umpire calls you out.

You walk slowly back to the dugout, rubbing your shoulder. "Wow, what a pitcher," you say to your teammates ruefully.

"Yeah, that must have been quite a throw to break the bat like that," says your third baseman, Muskrat Henderson.

"You're telling me," you say. "I think the trouble with Clinton's sinker is that even if we manage to hit it, there's nothing we can do with it." You're thinking that it's going to be a long afternoon of jarred shoulders and weak grounders for the Wynona Cougars.

"Well, we'll have to see if he can keep it up for the whole game," Brenda comments.

You shake your head. "I sure hope not."

Go on to the next page.

The next two innings remain scoreless. In the top of the fourth, the Pirates' Frank Murtha hits a single and then steals second. Their cleanup hitter Bye Bye Biner steps up to the plate.

The count goes to 2–2. On the next pitch Biner connects, and the ball goes rocketing out toward Wendy at first base. She goes after it, but the ball catches her on the hip and bounces off toward extreme right field. An error!

Turn to page 34.

Tully is furious when he realizes what has happened. You go out and try to calm him down, but it doesn't do much good. He's so distracted that he walks the next two batters, Darryl Vooch and Clinton, and has to face the top of the order with two runners on base and only one out.

For a while things go from bad to worse. Kayo Santucci singles to left. Then Toyota Turner bunts. The ball goes right out to the mound.

Tully grabs the ball in a fury and throws it way over Wendy's head. It sails out along the foul line and bumps against the railing. Suddenly that fat fan with the Yankees hat leaps out and grabs it again!

This time he takes a bow and gets a standing ovation before clambering back into the stands. You notice several security guards coming down the aisle to meet him.

The umpire gives everybody an extra base, and the score is 5–0, but you can see that Tully has calmed down. In fact, he seems downright amused by the whole escapade. Murtha hits into a double play, and you're out of the inning.

Turn to page 49.

This brings up Vooch with no one on base and two outs. He hits a home run to left field, and just like that you're behind again.

Finally, Tully strikes out Kravitz to end the side.

Kravitz continues to look awesome in the bottom of the ninth. But Rhubarb gets a small piece of one of his pitches and sends the ball whizzing over Good Dog McGee's head. Rhubarb winds up safe at first, and it's your turn at bat. You look at the first pitch, or at least you try to look at it, and decide to go down swinging.

On the second pitch, you take a blind cut, and to your astonishment, you connect. The ball goes rocketing out toward right field. Murtha gets a glove on it and deflects it slightly. You see it roll out into the far corner. Toyota Turner is giving chase, but out of the corner of your eye, you can see that she's having trouble.

It's a sure double, but you think there's a decent chance you could make third. Still, when the game is this close, you don't really want to risk an out. Maybe you'd be better off holding up at second. Rhubarb has crossed the plate, and the score is tied at 11–11. You only have a split second to make your decision.

*If you go for the triple,
turn to page 60.*

*If you decide to stop at second base,
turn to page 102.*

You signal for another fastball, and Tully burns one in, low and inside. Clinton takes a strike. Your mind wanders as you signal for the third fastball. You're trying to remember who's going to lead off for your side in the bottom of the ninth. The pitch comes in—and Clinton smacks it into deep right field!

You can't believe your eyes. T.T. is playing a little shallow and you can tell that he can't believe it either. In fact he's so surprised when the ball sails over his head that he trips over his own feet and falls as he's turning around to chase it.

Clinton sees T.T. fall as he's rounding first, and he puts on a burst of speed. He's on his way to third before T.T. gets the ball and throws. Clinton looks like he might just beat the ball to third—but then he makes the clumsiest slide you've ever seen. He starts too early and doesn't tuck his lower leg quite right. The slide peters out about a foot from the bag, and Muskrat actually has to reach forward to tag him out.

What an incredible blunder—Clinton never should have tried to take third. What's more, when he gets up, he is limping. The Scarboro manager rushes out onto the field. Clinton limps around in circles a bit, trying to walk it off. But it doesn't get any better. They're going to have to replace him. This could be just the break your team is looking for!

Turn to page 30.

98

You send Percy in as leadoff hitter in the bottom of the sixteenth inning. Clinton is just as tired as anyone else by now. But to his credit, he takes Percy to a full count.

Percy knows what that means. On the next pitch, he crowds in until his toes are almost touching home plate. Clinton is so unsettled by this that he throws the ball over catcher Vooch's head, and Percy is on with a walk.

When he gets to first base, he doesn't even take a lead—no sense giving the trick away. Clinton ignores him and goes into a full windup. But before he even reaches the stretch, Percy bolts like a startled deer.

His speed is truly amazing. Nothing happens until he's about three steps from second base. Then Vooch jumps up, pointing his finger and screaming at Clinton. Clinton, confused, glances over at first, where he sees nothing.

Turn to page 18.

Then the trouble starts. Toyota Turner comes to bat, and Tully throws a wild pitch that hits her in the shin. She takes her base. Then Frank Murtha connects on the very next pitch for a solid single, advancing Turner to third. Biner steps up to the plate.

"Come on, Tully, let's have a strikeout here," Muskrat Henderson yells encouragingly from third. "He's no batter!"

But you know Muskrat is wrong—Biner has already proven himself one of the Pirates' best sluggers. With two runners on base, you're afraid that this could be a big play for them. You signal for Tully's fast curveball. Tully delivers, and Biner swings and connects, but the ball goes foul along the left field line. A sigh goes up from the crowd.

"All right, Tully, let's see some more of that stuff!" yells Brian. "We need an out here!"

On the next pitch, Biner fouls again. And on the next. On the fourth pitch, he pops a high short foul up by the Scarboro dugout. If you can catch it, the inning will be over. You whip off your mask and dash over, concentrating on the ball. The Scarboro players yell at you, trying to break your concentration. But you ignore them and wait calmly until the ball drops neatly into your mitt. The Scarboro players fall silent. The inning is over, with no score.

Turn to page 73.

Cecil is already charging down the third base line. But you frantically wave him back. He looks at you as though he thinks you've lost your mind, but he goes back to third base. Only then do you look for the ball and see that Cecil could have scored easily.

You have made a big error in judgment. You try to forget it as you continue your turn at bat, but it won't leave your mind. It distracts you so much that you strike out on four pitches.

In the top of the fifth, Scarboro increases its lead to 5–0. By the bottom of the ninth the score is 14–0. You look back on your conservative play in the bottom of the fourth and wonder if that was the turning point of the game. Even if it was, there's not much you can do about it now. You have lost the championship.

The End

You stop at second with a stand-up double. The score is tied at 11–11 with no outs. You are the winning run. But Caveman Kravitz is determined to keep you from scoring. He strikes out Brian, Wendy, and Brenda, one after the other.

The Scarboro manager sends in a pinch hitter for Santucci in the top of the tenth, a tall skinny guy named Tony Peepers. You wonder what's wrong with Santucci. Peepers's strike zone is huge. Lots of possibilities, you think. But he smashes Tully's first pitch right back toward the mound. Tully just misses it, and the ball catches a corner of second base and pops up into the air. Before it comes down, Peepers is on first.

Turn to page 113.

You signal for Brenda to swing. She steps into the box. Clinton goes into his stretch and throws. It's a big fat sinking fastball, right over the plate. You can see Brenda's eyes widen as she steps into it and connects.

The ball whistles straight at Clinton, and for a second you think it might hit him in the head. But you don't have time to wait and see—you've got a run to score. In fact, all three runners are off at the crack of the bat. What happens next takes less than three seconds and is one of the rarest plays in baseball.

For some reason, out in center field Biner has decided to come in closer for this pitch. When the ball is hit on its low, straight trajectory, he's in the process of adjusting his position, trotting toward shallow center. The instant he sees the ball leave the bat, he breaks into a sprint.

Turn to page 16.

You go out to the mound to tell Tully that you're pulling him from the game. You've never had to do this before, and you're not sure how he'll take it. You're trying to figure out what to say when Tully exclaims, "Am I glad to see you! That McGee guy never should have hit my curve."

"Yeah, I guess it's time for a little fresh blood out here," you say, feeling relieved.

"You know I hate to be a quitter," Tully says sadly. "But I sure don't want to lose this one for the rest of you."

"No problem. Wishbone'll freeze these losers good."

But you're wrong about that. Wishbone immediately gives up a walk, two singles, and a triple, bringing the score to 10–5. By the end of the inning, it's 13–5. The Cougars go down in order in the bottom of the ninth. The game is over, and you lose.

The End

106

You whip the ball down to third. Muskrat grabs it and applies the tag. But it's close . . . and . . . Biner's slide knocks the ball free! It skips off into foul territory.

Seeing the loose ball, Biner jumps up and scores. The game goes to 2–0. "Good try," Wendy calls from first base. "We'll get him next time."

You hope she's right. Muskrat is scowling and shaking his head, looking angry with himself. You can only hope that he doesn't waste time brooding over the unsuccessful play. Muskrat is a solid hitter and a brilliant fielder as long as he keeps his attention on the game, but he's easily distracted.

You turn your attention back to Tully. The next batter, Joe Scover, hits a short fly out to center field. Byron has to race in to get it. It's close. He dives—and grabs the ball inches above the grass. The inning is over. But something seems to be wrong with Byron. He winces as he tosses the ball back to the infield. He must have hurt himself making that diving catch.

Turn to page 40.

You shake your head. "Never."

"Well, near as I can tell from the rule book, we have to treat this as an act of nature, like rain or snow. We may have to call the game. And I'm inclined to do it right now. If we do, the Cougars will win because it's after the fifth inning and they're leading."

"Wait a minute," says the Scarboro manager. "How do I know this isn't some kind of trick? What if Denby has pigeon juice in his hip pocket or something?"

"League rules state that if you can prove it anytime within a year after the game, you win by default," says the ump.

Then he turns to you. "Meanwhile, it says right here that the game can be continued at the discretion of the manager of the team that would win, in the interests of sportsmanship and the greater good of organized baseball. I guess that means you've got a decision to make."

With a couple of words, you can end the game and win the national championship! On the other hand, you'd really like to see how this one ends. With a 5–1 lead, you can probably afford to be a good sport. The ump and the Scarboro manager stare at you, awaiting your decision.

If you agree to end the game,
turn to page 45.

If you decide to keep playing,
turn to page 74.

108

Out on the field, as the announcer reads off the rosters with a flourish, you sneak a look at the Passyunk bullpen where Hackmore is warming up. Even from across the field you can tell he's going to be tough.

The head umpire calls you and the Passyunk manager over to home plate. He goes over a few ground rules for the park. You pull out the two lineup cards and glance at them, still trying to decide which one you want to use.

If you want to stick with your talented right-handers, turn to page 20.

If you decide to play a couple of your best lefties, turn to page 6.

Scarboro picks up a run in the eighth on a homer by Scover. You fail to score in your half of the inning, so it's 5–4 going into the top of the ninth.

Three more outs and you're the champs! But first you've got to get by Santucci, Turner, Murtha, and maybe Biner.

Santucci leads off the top of the ninth with a long single out to right center. He makes the turn at first and comes around, looking to see if he can get to second ahead of the throw. Brenda cuts off the ball and makes the best throw she can, but it dribbles to a stop twenty feet short of the bag. Seeing this, Santucci cruises into second.

In all the commotion of her grand slam, you forgot that Brenda has always been a weak fielder. And when you sent her in for Byron you also forgot that Brenda was coming back from a recent injury herself—she fell off a horse a few months ago, breaking her wrist. It's almost completely healed now, but her throwing is more erratic than ever. Now that you have a lead late in the game, you realize that Brenda's fielding problems could be a big liability. You'll have to take her out of the game.

Turn to page 13.

You send Mitch in for T.T. in right field. The next batter is Toyota Turner. Tully has been striking her out on breaking balls, so you signal for him to give her more of the same. On the second pitch, Turner bunts.

You field it and throw her out, but Santucci advances to third. With only one out, you know that he'll score easily on any kind of sacrifice.

The next batter up for the Pirates is their star slugger, Frank Murtha. Murtha strides confidently up to the plate. Tully's first pitch goes wide. You signal for a curveball, hoping for the best—you know that Murtha is the kind of batter who can hit virtually anything.

Tully winds up and throws. Murtha swings and connects. It's a long high drive down the first base line. It looks as if it's going to go foul. Mitch is racing over. If he catches this foul, Santucci can tag up and score, tying the game! But Mitch is a born catcher, accustomed to grabbing every pop foul he can—he may not know he should drop this one. Should you yell out for him to drop it, or just sit tight and trust his judgment?

*If you yell instructions to Mitch,
turn to page 26.*

*If you keep quiet,
turn to page 66.*

112

Brian is up next. He hits a sharp grounder to Santucci at second base. You take off like a shot, but you have to slow down to avoid the batted ball. Then you dive for the bag. It all happens in a split second. As you're sliding into second, you hear a roar go up from the crowd as Rhubarb reaches third.

The bases are loaded! Wendy steps up to the plate, looking determined. She swings at the first pitch, hitting a grounder up the middle. The ball takes a bad hop and flies high in the air. Scover is backpedaling, but he sees that he's going to have to turn and chase it. That's your opening!

Rhubarb breaks for the plate. An instant later, Scover spins to throw home. Vooch is blocking the plate. Rhubarb barrels into him, knocking him onto his back. But Vooch has deflected Rhubarb's momentum, and he slides past the plate on his belly. Somehow he manages to reach out and catch a corner of the plate as he goes by. You win! You're the champs!

The End

After that, Turner and Murtha hit a triple and a homer back-to-back, and the score is 14–11. A few minutes later Scover hits Biner home, bringing the score to 15–11. By that time, the game is out of reach. Your side goes down 1–2–3 in the bottom of the tenth. It doesn't even occur to you until the plane ride home to wonder whether it would have made any difference if you had stretched that double to a triple.

The End

You decide to cool it. Yelling at the umpire and possibly getting thrown out of the game isn't going to do anybody any good.

"C'mon, the game's tied. We've got our work cut out for us," says Tully soothingly. He pulls you back toward the plate. "We can still win here. Those Pirates are no match for us." When play resumes, it seems that he might be right. You retire the next batter successfully. All you need to do to win is score one run.

But Lionel Bax and his big jughandle curve are too much for your batters. He holds you off in the bottom of the ninth.

In the top of the tenth, Scarboro scores a run on a walk, a stolen base, a sacrifice, and a suicide squeeze. Right away, your mind takes the positive. You start planning how to catch them in the bottom of the inning. But then Biner comes up to bat and smashes a home run on Tully's very first pitch. The score is 7–5.

You struggle to hold on to your positive thoughts. There's still a chance you could overcome a 7–5 deficit. Then Scover and Good Dog McGee hit back-to-back singles. By the end of the inning the score is 8–5. Your weakest batters have to face Lionel Bax for the first time—and overcome a three-run deficit. It's a tall order, and they fail to meet it. It was a long game, and you gave it your best shot. You're glad it's over.

The End

ABOUT THE AUTHOR

FELIX VON MOSCHZISKER is a graduate of Yale University and a lifelong baseball fan. At the start of his career, he worked as a journalist for the *Philadelphia Evening Bulletin*, the Time-Life News Service, and *Life* magazine. Since then, he has started his own newspaper as well as a string of informational publications for the vacation community where he lives in Vermont. And a few years ago, he launched a modestly successful second career as an abstract sculptor in bronze and marble. He is a bicyclist in summer and a skier in winter.

ABOUT THE ILLUSTRATOR

HAL FRENCK studied at Syracuse University. He has worked at several advertising companies, most recently BBDO in New York. Mr. Frenck has illustrated books for many different publishers, including *Earthquake!* and *Playoff Champion* in the Bantam Choose Your Own Adventure series. He lives in Fairfield, Connecticut.

CHOOSE YOUR OWN ADVENTURE